JUST
LIKE DAVID

BY MARGUERITE de ANGELI

jD345ju

THE JUNIOR LITERARY GUILD AND

DOUBLEDAY & COMPANY, INC., GARDEN CITY, NEW YORK

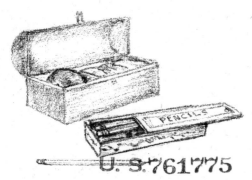

This book is for
Jeffrey.
It is for David too
and for Henry.

1   Jeffrey stood watching for David to come home. Nearly always, David had something to tell that he had learned in school. But this time it was Jeffrey who had something to tell. Something exciting. Something David didn't know. As he waited, he pushed at his front tooth. He was sure it felt loose. He hoped so. It would make him feel almost as big as David.

David was seven. Jeffrey was five and a half. Henry was still younger. He wasn't even two. David, Jeffrey, and Henry lived with Mother and Daddy near Hatboro, just outside Philadelphia.

David came around the bend of the road, kicking the dry leaves ahead of him.

"Guess what?" said Jeffrey, running to meet him. "We're going to move away from here!"

"Away from Hatboro?" asked David.

"Yes," nodded Jeffrey. "We're going to Ohio to live."

David looked to see if Jeffrey kept his mouth straight or whether his eyes looked ready to laugh. Sometimes Jeffrey made up outrageous stories that were only fooling.

6

But David could always tell when he was fooling, because Jeffrey couldn't keep his face straight. So he said, "Put your mouth!"

This time Jeffrey kept his mouth firm and straight, just as David did, so David had to believe him.

"When?" he said.

"Daddy says next week," answered Jeffrey. "He just called Mother. He says the letter just came from his friend Bill. Remember when Daddy went out to Ohio on the train?"

7

David nodded. He frowned, too. He wasn't at all certain he wanted to move away from home and go somewhere else to school. Away from his teacher, Miss Torrey. Just when it was time for the Halloween party, too. And just when Miss Torrey had begun to read Treasure Island.

"Mother says Daddy's bought us a new house," Jeffrey went on. "So now we can't have a new car."

"A house? And no new car?" David frowned again.

Jeffrey didn't notice the frown. He felt too important because he had surprised David. He stretched up as tall as possible, trying to look as much like David as he could. He wanted to do everything just like David. He wanted to go to school, too, and to learn to read as David did. He had been all ready to begin school in September. Daddy had brought him a pencil box and Mother had taken him to school herself. But the school had been too crowded. The teacher could accept only children who had passed their sixth birthday. Jeffrey had been very disappointed. But now he had something new to think about.

By the following week everybody and everything was all ready to go to Ohio. The van had taken the furniture and the boys'

things. David had packed his play garage and his box of paints and crayons. Jeffrey had put in his sailboat and the little Japanese house and his pencil box. For Daddy had said when they were alone, "Perhaps when we get to Ohio you'll need your pencil box. We'll see 'if.' You and I will keep that for a secret, shall we?" After that Jeffrey was more excited than ever about moving.

Now the house stood bare and empty, and not like home any more. The family was in the car. Henry sat in his little canvas chair between Daddy and Mother on the front seat. David and Jeffrey shared the back seat with things they would need on the journey. It was rather crowded. There was a pile of coats on the seat and a lunch basket. On the floor was a large suitcase, Daddy's briefcase, his camera, and a bag of apples. On the shelf back of the seat were several packages, tissues, a flash-light, two books, and a number of small things that Mother had put in at the last minute. Some of the packages were secret presents from Grandpa. "To be opened when you just can't stand it any longer," he had said. Jeffrey had felt them, but he couldn't guess.

All the neighborhood children stood be-side the car, waiting to say good-by.

David didn't want to leave Marshall, who
was his best friend. They had such fun in the
woods together. Besides, it was Halloween,
and they wouldn't be able to go with the children to collect "cold pieces." But he did want
to see what Ohio looked like.

Jeffrey didn't want to leave Rita, his best

friend, but he liked to ride in the car. Besides, there was that secret something exciting that might happen in Ohio. Daddy had said, "If."

Henry didn't want to leave Mother. Not even long enough for her to get things straight before they started. He clung to her coat collar and walked on her lap.

Daddy put his foot on the starter. "Here we go!" he said.

The motor growled and stuttered.

"Good-by, Rita! Good-by, Nancy! Good-by, Marshall! Good-by! Good-by!"

The motor roared, but nothing happened. The car stood still. Mother looked anxiously at Daddy as he got out and lifted the hood.

Daddy twisted something under the hood, and asked Mother to push the starter. The motor roared. Daddy got into the car.

13

"Out of the way, boys," he called. He put the car in gear, and off it went.

"Good-by!" called David.

"Good-by!" called Jeffrey.

"'By!" said Henry, and Mother and Daddy called good-by too.

"Good-by!" said Rita and Nancy. "Good-by!" said Marshall and all the other children. "Good-by, good-by, good-by, good-by . . ." The last good-by sounded far off.

"Now," said David, "we are really going."

14

"Is it a long way to Ohio?" asked Jeffrey.

"Way?" questioned Henry.

"It's as far as two days and staying somewhere overnight two times," said Mother. "We are late getting started, so we'll stay at Aunt Ginny's tonight."

On the way through Hatboro, they passed the sign with the hat on it. David almost knew the sign by heart because he saw it often. He read one side, which said, "Hatboro, so named because hats were manufactured here as early as 1705. During the revolution they were made for the Continental troops." Then, as they rode on, he looked back and read the other side of the sign, which said, "Hatboro, the site of the Battle of the Crooked Billet."

Jeffrey looked at the sign, too, and waved. Ohio seemed much more exciting.

16

HATBORO
FOUNDED 1705
SITE of
BATTLE
of the
CROOKED
BILLET
HATBORO
1705

Suddenly Jeffrey said, "I'm hungry."

David said, "So am I," and Henry said, "I, I." So Mother gave them each an apple.

"We'll eat supper at Aunt Ginny's," she said, "so be patient."

Daddy drove around the city to the road leading west. They went through a place called "Gwynedd." Mother said it was a Welsh name, and that the early settlers there had come from Wales.

They went through several small towns, then through Valley Forge Park.

"This is where Washington and the Continental troops spent the winter during the Revolution," said Daddy. "When we get up on the hill you can see the little huts where they lived through those bitter months."

"I know about that," David said. "It's in our reader how they almost starved to death and froze."

Jeffrey was glad that he knew about George Washington, too. There was a picture of him in an oval frame at Grandma's near the bed where Jeffrey slept. In the picture Washington had white hair and wore it in a long twist with a bow. Grandma said it was a "queue." She had said George Washington was the first President of our country.

As they drove up over the hill, they saw

little log huts not much bigger than Grandpa's tool shed. Red leaves from the dogwood trees and from the maples sifted down in the late afternoon sunlight. It looked pretty, but it looked lonesome too. Farther down over the hill was an old tavern and a stone house.

"That little stone house was Washington's headquarters," Daddy said. "That is where he lived and where he talked with the officers

and wrote letters to Congress begging for supplies."

Sometimes Jeffrey didn't know just what Daddy meant, but he knew about Congress, because one day they had all gone to Philadelphia to Independence Hall. Daddy had told the boys how men from all the thirteen colonies had met to talk about making this a new country. They had called the meeting a "congress."

As they left Valley Forge, the road climbed higher along the crest of a hill. On each side were farms with large barns and hencoops, apple orchards and spreading fields. There were cows standing waiting to be milked, and sheep grazing. Sometimes there were signs offering things for sale. David read them aloud as they passed. One sign said: HAY, STRAW & VINEGAR. It made a nice sound.

Jeffrey began to chant it, and David joined in: "Hay, straw, and vinegar; hay, straw and vinegar; hay-straw 'n vinegar," over and over, till Daddy said, "That's enough."

Then they saw a sign that read: APPLE JELLY & COLLIE PUPS, and another that read: LACE DOILIES & CANARIES, which set them giggling.

The boys knew about apple jelly. They had had it for breakfast. But what were "collie pups"? Jeffrey wanted to know.

"Little curly baby dogs," said Mother.

"And what are 'doilies'?" asked David.

"Little linen or lace pieces such as Grandma has on her sideboard," explained Mother.

"I know about canaries," said Jeffrey. "Mrs. Murphy had one. She kept it in a cage, and it sang and sang."

"Sang and sang," echoed Henry, teetering

from one foot to the other on Mother's lap. He rubbed his eyes and pulled at his ear, as he did when he was sleepy.

"If you boys will be quiet," Mother said, "I think somebody will go to sleep." She held Henry in her arms and sang a quiet song about all the baby things going to sleep. The birds in their nests, the chickadees, the swallows under the eaves, the pussycats in the kitchen, calves and colts in the barnyard, and collie pups. Go-ing-to-sleep.

There was so much to see that in no time at all they were far from the city and Daddy was saying, "Now we are in Lancaster County."

2   The sun was low now, and long
shadows stretched across the hills and fields.

The farms were very neat and tidy. The
fields looked like the patches on a quilt, Jeffrey thought. One, far up on the hill, was like
the tufted coverlets on the boys' beds. Some
were brown squares with gold stripes where

there was stubble left from the wheat. Some were bright green where new wheat or rye had been planted. It would stay in the ground all winter, then begin to grow again after the snow was gone. Some of the patches were dark purple where the soil was rich and it had been plowed.

A barn stood close to the road as they went around a curving hill.

"Look!" said Jeffrey. "It has pictures on it." And there under the eaves were bright painted whorls, and stars in circles. There were bright bands around the tall windows that looked like shutters.

"Why are all the windows closed?" asked David.

"They aren't really closed," said Daddy. "They are really open. Those are louvers or slatted openings to let in air so the hay won't spoil. Soon we'll see tobacco barns. They will have long, loose boards that swing out from the top to let in air. This is great tobacco country."

Farther along the road, they met a boy carrying a pail. He wasn't much older than Jeffrey. He wore a big black hat and his hair was bobbed. He wore high black shoes and a purple shirt, and his trousers came about halfway down to his ankles.

"Amish," said Daddy, "or some call them German Quakers."

Each farm seemed more beautiful than the last. Jeffrey thought the fields looked as if they had been embroidered and tied down at the edges to keep them smooth. There were great barns much larger than the houses. Just as Daddy had said, there were tobacco barns with long boards swinging outward.

Once, when they were not far from Lancaster, they saw women cooking outdoors. They were stirring something in a great iron kettle.

"Making apple butter," said Daddy even before Jeffrey had time to ask.

"Like we have for breakfast?"

"The very same," answered Daddy.

Then they saw a sign which said: APPLE BUTTER & SNITZ FOR SALE, so they stopped. Mother bought a large jar of apple butter and some cider.

"What is 'snitz'?" asked David, pointing to the sign.

"Pared and sliced apples," said Daddy again. "Snitz means cut and dried apples, or just sliced apples."

Henry woke up. "Apples?" he questioned.

"No, not now," Mother said. "Soon we'll be at Aunt Ginny's. Then we'll have supper and go to bed."

Then Mother told the boys to look for the tall chimneys and the water tower of Lancaster.

Soon the dark chimneys began to appear.

"Now it won't be long till we're there. And we'll see Jean," said Jeffrey. Jean's birthday was not long after Jeffrey's.

It was almost dark when they drew up in front of the house. There was a bright light in the window, and tall Uncle Bill and Aunt

Ginny and Jean were on the porch to greet
them.

Supper was ready by the time Henry was
fed and put to bed. Jean, David, and Jeffrey
sat at the small table.

"You know what?" asked Jean. "Henry is going to have my tricycle, and you can take it in the car."

So when they left next morning early, the tricycle went into the car with the extra coats, the suitcases and the lunch basket, the brief-case, the camera, and the apples. This time there was a can of pretzels, which Uncle Bill said they must take. He always got them at a special place in Lititz. Jeffrey loved the salty taste — but even better he liked what Jean had told them.

"Do you know why pretzels are made in this shape?" she had said. "Long, long ago, it was made to represent a good child. Like this —" She had crossed her arms on her breast with her eyes down.

Aunt Ginny had packed a lunch for them.

It was chilly as they rode along in the early morning on their way toward Harrisburg. Just ahead was the interchange where they would go onto the Pennsylvania Turnpike. The farmhouses and the houses in the little towns began to be different. Instead of plastered stone, they were of red brick. Nearly every house had an upstairs porch.

"Wouldn't it be fun to play up there, on that porch?" Jeffrey asked. "We could make believe it was a ship or something. I wish we had something exciting to do now."

"Can we see the secrets?" begged David.

"Can we? Can we?" Jeffrey grabbed Mother around the neck from the back, while Henry dragged at her coat collar from the front.

"Oh, no, not yet." Mother spoke as well as she could.

"What can we do, then?" Jeffrey teased.

"Sit down," said Mother. "You're choking me. Look at all the things we're passing. We still have all day today and all day tomorrow to ride. Play a game, you two. See how many kettle houses you can count before we come to the turnpike."

"What's a kettle house?" Jeffrey asked.

"It's a special house where there are big copper kettles for cooking apple butter or boiling clothes."

"How can we play that when Jeff can't count?" David asked, scowling.

"I can too," said Jeffrey. "To a hundred!"

"Well, you can't read, and I can," David
boasted.

"Maybe I can when I get to Ohio," said
Jeffrey, squirming from side to side as he
always did. David looked scornful. But Jeffrey thought of the secret he and Daddy had.
"If," he said to himself happily. Then he began to chant, "We're going on the turnpike,
going on the turnpike."

Soon Daddy said, "That's enough."

Before they had gone forty miles the kettle houses began to disappear. Black chimneys and foundries of a steel plant looked up. There were steep streets lined with close-set houses, rather dark from the smoke of the foundries.

Before long the car turned onto another road and they were in Harrisburg.

"We haven't time to stop," said Daddy, "but as we ride along, I want you to look up the streets to the right. You can see the dome of the State House. Harrisburg is the capital of Pennsylvania, the state where you have always lived until now."

"What's capital?" Jeffrey wanted to know. "And what's a state?"

"I'll explain," said Mother, setting Henry down in his little chair. She got out the map

to show David and Jeffrey what the state of
Pennsylvania looks like. She pointed out
Harrisburg and the way they had come from
home near Philadelphia.

Then she went on to explain that the capital of a state is the city where the governor
lives and where the laws are made.

"What's the governor?" inquired Jeffrey.

"He's something like the father in a family.
He helps to make the laws and shows people
the right way to live. We have to have laws
because some people won't live by the
Golden Rule. You know what that is."

"Do unto others as you want them to do unto you," said both boys at once.

"That's it," said Mother. "So, you see, when people vote to say who shall be governor, they have to be careful to choose a good one."

"Is there a governor in Ohio?" asked Jeffrey.

"Of course," said David, just as if he had always known. "Every state has a governor, doesn't it, Daddy?"

Daddy nodded. He was too busy to talk because the traffic was heavy.

"Are we near to Ohio?" asked Jeffrey, wishing he could tell what the big letters said on the front of the large building they were passing.

"LIBRARY," David said.

"Not very near," said Mother. "But soon we will be on the turnpike. Then we can go

without having to stop for lights and crossroads. We can go without stopping, unless
the car gives out. After we leave the turnpike,
it is only about two hours until we reach
Ohio."

Jeffrey clapped his hands. "Oh, goody,
then we'll be at our new house, won't we?"

"Mercy, no," answered Mother. "It will take all afternoon to go over the turnpike. Then we'll have to stop for supper and stay overnight someplace. Tomorrow we shall have to drive nearly all day before we come to our house. It's away across Ohio, you know, right near Cincinnati, and right on the Ohio River."

"All day?" Jeffrey couldn't believe they could ride all day for two whole days and still not come to the edge of the world. He remembered that he was hungry. "Can't we have our picnic now?" he asked. By that time they were going over a long bridge that crossed a wide, shallow river.

"Is this the Ohio River?" he asked again.

"No, silly, of course not," said David. "What river is it, Daddy?"

"This is the Susquehanna," Mother an-

swered. "It flows for a long way and into the Chesapeake Bay below Philadelphia. Susquehanna is an Indian name. There used to be lots of Indians here, you know. In that old diary we have, it tells how one of my great-grandmothers was held captive by the Indians for almost a year. They were kind to her, though, and she grew to be fond of them. Then her father found her and brought her home again."

"Lived with real Indians?" Jeffrey wondered what it would be like to live in a tepee like the picture in David's book. Then he remembered again that he was hungry.

"When can we eat the picnic you brought, Mother?"

"When we get well out into the country," Mother promised, "and just before we go onto the turnpike. It won't be long."

And it wasn't long before Daddy said, "Keep your eyes open, boys. It is nearly time for us to be going onto the turnpike. You'll see a lot of trucks lined up at the filling station, and we'll stop there, too. We'll make sure everything is all right and that everyone is comfortable. There are long stretches on the turnpike without gas stations. I just hope the car holds up. It might be awkward to limp along the turnpike, because the cars go fast there." And just then the filling station came into view. Daddy drew up to the gas pump, and the attendant began to work on the car.

"Now, everybody out. Stretch your legs and be ready for the long ride over the turnpike." Mother helped Henry down.

"Down?" he said.

At the woods' edge there were a table and benches just for travelers to use. While the man was attending to the car, they ate lunch. They emptied both thermos bottles, so Daddy took them into the lunchroom to be refilled, one with milk and one with coffee. Daddy brought ice-cream cones, too. Henry enjoyed his so thoroughly that even his ears had to be washed.

When the car had been serviced, Mother helped put things in order again on the back seat. The boys changed places, and Daddy started off.

"What is the turnpike?" asked Jeffrey.

"A road on which there are tollgates," ex-

plained Daddy. "The toll is used to keep the road in repair and to pay the men who collect it. 'Toll' is a tax of money. When we get to the gate we'll be given a ticket with the names of all the interchanges printed on it. The ticket will be punched at the gate where we enter. When we leave the turnpike we pay a certain amount, depending on how far we have gone. Understand?"

Jeffrey nodded. "Like Mother at the supermarket?" he wanted to know.

"Yes, something like that. She pays for the number of things she has bought. On the turnpike we pay for the number of miles we have gone. You know, this is one of the greatest roads in the country. It goes for hundreds of miles without intersections or crossroads. There are no advertising signs to spoil the landscape. And all the places to stop for food and gas are well built and attractive."

"Oh," said Jeffrey. But to him it still looked like just a wide road with a grassy strip in the middle.

"Oh," echoed Henry, nodding too. Everybody laughed.

They rolled onto the overpass leading into

the turnpike. In a moment they passed under the shelter at the tollgate, where a man gave them a ticket. It was punched, just as Daddy had said, at the place where they had entered.

"When we leave the turnpike for the regular highway," said Daddy, "we'll pass through another tollgate. But that won't be for a long time. Probably we shall spend the night in Washington, Pennsylvania. That is, we will if the car keeps going." He sighed.

Jeffrey knew how much Daddy had wanted to buy a new car. They had all wanted it. When they had given up the thought of a new car, Daddy had said, "We have to choose what is best. When we get to Ohio we have to have a house and new things to go into it. Besides, it costs a great deal to move all our things. So we'll just have to make the old car do for a while."

As it chuffed along, Mother asked anxiously, "Isn't the car running all right?"

"It isn't hitting on all six," answered Daddy. "Hear that?"

Jeffrey didn't know what "hitting on all six" meant, but he knew that the motor wasn't running smoothly. He said, "Listen, David, it goes purr-r-r, ptt, ptt, purr-r-r, ptt, ptt."

David said, "No, it goes like this—m-m-m-

46

p-pst, m-m-m-p-pst." They both kept up their own version of the sound until Mother asked them to stop.

David began to wonder what Marshall was doing, and whether the boys had found his secret hidey-hole in the big tree. Jeffrey wondered if Rita was swinging on the gate as they used to do, waiting for the children to come from school. It seemed long ago, but it had been only yesterday. He began to tease Henry, who giggled and jumped around on Mother's lap. David joined in, so that all three boys were dodging and bumping around Mother's head. Once David's head bumped into Jeffrey's mouth and made his front tooth even looser. They got louder and louder till Mother cried, "Stop it! Please!" But they scarcely heard her and kept on giggling.

Then Daddy spoke. "That's enough!"

They quieted. Then Mother said, "Why
don't you watch for the tunnel?"

"Tunnel?" David and Jeffrey jumped up
on the back seat to look out. David saw the
sign warning them to SLOW DOWN. They
had to fall in line behind a big truck that
rumbled slowly into the light of the tunnel.

48

David read the large letters over the entrance. They spelled BLUE MOUNTAIN. And inside it did seem blue.

"Are we under the mountain?" Jeffrey asked in wonder.

"Right under," said Daddy. "But it is solid rock, so it won't fall in."

In a few moments they came out into daylight again and the sunshine looked very bright.

But before Jeffrey could say "wink" they were in another tunnel!

Daddy drove the car around mountains, down into deep curves, across wide-spreading valleys, and through several more tunnels. David always read the warning to SLOW DOWN — TUNNEL AHEAD, and always Jeffrey got as far as the "S" and couldn't read any more letters before they were past the sign. If only he could read like David!

Each time they went through a tunnel, Jeffrey said, "Is this Ohio?"

And always the answer was, "No, not yet."

When the weary old car puffed and grunted on the hills, Daddy urged it along saying, "Giddy-ap, Napoleon!"

David and Jeffrey helped, too, with "Giddy-ap, Napoleon," and Henry always echoed, "Gi' yap!"

It was lots of fun and somehow helped to get the car up the hill.

As the day grew older, the hills were higher.

Sometimes it looked as if the car couldn't get through. The mountains, bold and dark against the sky, seemed to close in the road. But each time it wound around and came out and went on again.

The hours dragged. David was weary of
reading signs. Jeffrey had seen enough of
trees and woods. He yawned and lay down
on the coats.

Even Mother looked tired. Then Daddy
pointed up at the steep sides where the road
had been cut through a hill.

"You see how these rocks are all standing on end?" he asked.

David slid forward to listen, and Jeffrey sat up.

"Millions of years ago, this land was all under water, sea water. Then the hot inner core of the earth began to move and change. And it pushed the top crust up in humps like that, just like the crust on Mother's apple pie."

"What's the core?" Jeffrey wanted to know.

"You know what the core of an apple is, don't you? And you know the earth is round like an apple?"

Jeffrey nodded.

"How do they know there was a sea?" asked David.

"By the fossils of marine life in the rocks," explained Daddy.

"What are fossils?"

"The remains of living things that have left their imprint in stone. Sometimes they find fern and fish patterns in coal. That is a kind of stone, too, and there is lots of coal in Pennsylvania. There is iron in these mountains, too, and deep down there are deposits of oil. All those things were used to make this wonderful road for us to ride on. And from the oil, we get gasoline to run the car and refined oil to keep the engine from getting too hot."

Suddenly David sang out, "Tunnel ahead, slow down, Napoleon!"

Jeffrey looked at the sign as it flashed by. He chuckled — because even he could see that "Napoleon" wasn't on it.

The car slowed down. The engine coughed because they were going uphill.

"Giddy-ap, Napoleon, giddy-ap, Napoleon." Daddy urged the car up the rise and through the long tunnel. But on the other side of the tunnel the road continued to rise, and the car went more and more slo-w-l-y. Steam rose in a cloud from the radiator and hissed loudly. Daddy managed to steer the car into one of the bays at the side before it stopped altogether. There he could get out safely to look under the hood. Mother didn't say a word, but she looked anxious.

When Daddy got back into the car and tried the starter, it went a little — then it stopped. Daddy tried again. This time the engine really ran, but instead of going "pur-r-r-r-r," it went "pur-r-r-ptt, pr-r-r-ptt," like Rita's cat when it was angry.

"There's no help for it," said Daddy, sighing. "We've just got to stop and have the car fixed. I had hoped we could get to Ohio without buying the new core for the radiator that I know is needed, but we can't. The water keeps boiling up and over the engine. I only hope we can keep going to the next interchange. We can spend the night there instead of in Washington, Pennsylvania."

Mother sighed.

David wilted and groaned.

Jeffrey wiggled the loose tooth and said, "Isn't it Ohio yet?"

The car ran so jerkily and had to be stopped so often that it took some time to get to the tollgate at the interchange. But not far from the turnpike was a small town where Daddy found a garage.

Near by, too, was a fine tourist house where

Mother and the boys stayed while Daddy took the car to be repaired. The tourist house was set in a wide, grassy lawn with rows and rows of doors on two levels. Each door led into a bedroom, Mother said, and each room had its own bathroom. There was an outside stairway leading to the rooms on the second level. There was a platform halfway and steps leading down both to the front and to the back. It was a fine place to play ship.

"This is better than the upstairs porches near Lancaster," said David.

"And better than the kettle houses, hunh?" Jeffrey agreed. "Can I be the captain?"

"No," said David. "I'm the captain, because I'm the biggest, and go to school. I'm Captain Bill," he said in his most grown-up voice. "You're the first mate, Joe."

Jeffrey knew he had to be "Joe" if he

wanted to play. Sometimes at home they had played knights and castles. Sometimes they played cowboys and Indians. Or David made believe he was boss of a gas station and Jeffrey was his helper. But, whatever game they played, David was always the boss, "Bill," and Jeffrey was always "Joe." Jeffrey thought to himself, "When I go to school, I'll be 'Bill' and I'll say what we play. And I'll make David be 'Joe'."

Henry was a passenger, so it didn't matter whether he went up or down the stairs. The flashlight from the car made a splendid spyglass for Captain Bill, and the wheel of a faucet under the steps was very useful for First Mate Joe to guide the ship. He promised Mother that he wouldn't turn it even the least little bit.

When Daddy came back from the garage,

he said, "The car will be ready about nine in the morning."

It was past time for supper. There was a pleasant dining room near the tourist house, so Mother said they would save the food in the basket for the next day and would have a hot supper tonight.

"Can we eat in a restaurant?" asked Jeffrey, patting his hands together under his chin as he always did when he was excited.

"Restaurant it is!" said Daddy.

"Can we have whatever we want?" asked David. "Can we have ice cream?"

"Ice cream?" Henry danced in excitement.

"This once," said Mother. "You may choose whatever you like. Only you must eat it, remember."

It was fun eating in the restaurant and going to sleep in a tourist room. Henry was

to sleep between David and Jeffrey in a big bed. At first he kept climbing up and walking around. He stood on his head and looked through his legs at the boys. Even Mother and Daddy laughed, so he went through all his funny tricks to make them laugh more. At last Daddy said, "That's enough! Get ready to go to sleep."

Next morning Daddy got the car while Mother packed all the things they had needed for the night. They went again to the little restaurant for breakfast. David and Jeffrey remembered all their manners, and Henry was very good. He ate all of his cereal and didn't once put his dish on top of his head.

It was a very short distance to the turnpike, where they once more went through the toll-gate. They were given a ticket, as before, showing the place where they had entered.

"Now," said Daddy, "I hope we can keep going till we get to our house."

The old car chuffed along steadily but not very fast.

"Go fast, Daddy," said Jeffrey. "I want to get there and see it. And I want to see — if — you know what, Daddy."

"But we are going as fast as we can," said Daddy. "Be patient. Suppose we had to go over these hills in covered wagons as the pioneers did. It would take us weeks."

Jeffrey slid forward again. He remembered

the picture over Daddy's desk. It showed a long line of covered wagons drawn by oxen. The men carried muskets and wore broad-brimmed hats. The ladies wore bonnets and long dresses. Daddy had said they were "pioneers," making a trail to the West. It made it seem real to go over the same way. Jeffrey wondered how they ever got the big wagons over the mountains. It must be lonely there at night.

"Where did they sleep?" he asked, pulling at Mother's collar. "And where did they cook? Did they have a stove and everything?"

"They cooked over open fires, I guess. Or perhaps some of them had stoves they were moving to their new homes. Probably the women and the children slept in the wagons, and the men and the boys slept out by the campfire to keep watch."

"Why did they have to watch?" Jeffrey wanted to know.

"Because there were bears and Indians, silly," said David. "Don't you know anything? They put the wagons in a circle and made the camp inside, didn't they, Daddy?"

"That's what I've been told," Daddy agreed.

"Were they bad Indians?" Jeffrey questioned again.

"I don't know as they were bad, exactly,"

Mother explained. "If you had your home taken away from you as they had, and couldn't find enough food for your family, perhaps you would fight, too. In Pennsylvania there were many friendly Indians. Probably there were friendly Indians out West, too. We'll look it all up when we get home and find out." Mother laughed a little. "Home," she said. And Jeffrey knew she was thinking how funny it would be to call it "home" in Ohio.

In about two hours they left the turnpike and passed through the tollgate leading to the regular highway. Daddy let David pay the toll and count the change. David added the pennies, dimes, and quarters very quickly and gave the change to Daddy.

"Perhaps," Daddy said, "when we come this way again, you can count the change, Jeffrey." He winked to remind Jeffrey of their

secret. "If," he said.

"What do you mean, 'if'?" David asked.

Jeffrey clapped his hands. "It's our secret, isn't it, Daddy?"

David felt very important when the guard said, "There you are, sir. Have a good journey, sir." That gave him an idea, too.

"I know," he said. "Let's play tollgate.

Every time we go under a bridge, we'll make believe it's a tollgate. I'll be the man at the gate, and you be Joe, the man driving the car like Daddy."

Jeffrey was "Joe" again, "zoom-zooming" as if he were starting a car.

But there were no more bridges. There were twists and turns in a bad road, and hills and more hills.

Then suddenly Jeffrey was tired of "zoom-zooming." "I'm hungry," he said.

"Apples and pretzels!" said David. Then for a while there was great munching while everybody ate apples. Jeffrey gnawed at his apple very carefully because of his loose tooth. Even Daddy ate slices as Mother put them into his mouth while he drove.

"Snitz!" he said. Everybody laughed.

"Snitz!" said David.

"Snitz!" said Jeffrey.

"Snitz!" said Henry.

Then the road began to climb up, up, up.

"We're leaving West Virginia!" Daddy called out. "All aboard for Ohio."

"Leaving?" said David in astonishment. "I didn't know we were in it."

The boys climbed up to look. West Virginia didn't look very different.

"When we crossed the line a while back, I meant to tell you we were leaving our native state, but I forgot. We crossed only a narrow strip of West Virginia. Here we go!"

"What's a native state?" Jeffrey asked.

"Where you were born, silly," David said.

Down, down, down they went, across a bridge, and down, far, far below, was the river.

David read a sign that said — ENTERING OHIO.

3 "Is this where we live then?" queried Jeffrey.

"Oh, no," Mother said again. "Ohio is a large state like Pennsylvania, and the Ohio River runs a long, long way. We still have to ride all day to get to our house."

A barge was being towed down-river.

"Just think," Mother went on, "in a few days that barge will go right past our new house, won't it, Daddy? And maybe we'll be there to see it."

"Will we get there first?" asked Jeffrey, wiggling the loose tooth. It seemed as if it would be faster to go right down the river. Mother got out the map again. She showed the boys where they had just crossed a little corner of West Virginia.

"And here is where we are now," she pointed out. "This is where the road leads right across the state. The river, you see, winds far to the south. Besides, river travel is much slower than by car, even this car." She laughed.

As they left the river behind, Daddy shouted, "Hurrah for Ohio! This is our very own river and new state."

"Now we'll soon be at our new house, won't we?" Jeffrey said, confidently nodding his head up and down.

"House," said Henry, nodding, too, and jumping up and down on Mother's lap.

Mother sighed. "Tonight," was all she said.

Soon the country began to look somewhat different. Signs appeared offering pottery and china for sale. There were strange black towers shooting up into the air with seesaw things going up and down.

"Oil wells," said Daddy. "There is oil in Ohio, too, and pockets of natural gas. They just put a pipe down, and up comes the gas to burn for heat and for cooking."

They passed signs saying: CHEESE FOR SALE. The hills flattened out. Farmhouses dotted them. Not like the houses in Penn-

sylvania. There were no kettle houses, and no upstairs porches. The houses were of white frame, wide and homelike. Mother and Daddy talked about them and how different they were from Pennsylvania houses.

"You see," said Daddy, explaining, "the people who settled Ohio came here over a hundred years ago. They built their houses like those they came from in New York State and New England. You will see how most of the little towns have a center square with elms set about it. It's very pretty, I think. They named the towns after those they had left behind, too—Cambridge, New Concord, Norwich."

"Maybe they were lonesome," said David, wishing he could see Marshall.

"I don't see why," Jeffrey said. "I like Ohio."

Just as they were speaking, the road curved around and up into a village. There were the tall elm trees set about the square. There was a post office, a town hall, and stores where dry goods and groceries were sold. The drugstores had the same kinds of signs as the drugstore back home. Somehow, it seemed as if they were not quite so far from home when they saw those signs.

When they came out into the country again, there were fields of shocked corn standing in rows, such as they had seen before, but the way the hill rose made the shocks stand out against the sky.

"See the Indian tepees," said Daddy, nodding toward them.

"Put your mouth!" said David. "There aren't any Indians here . . . are there?" his voice suddenly questioned. For it seemed as if there might be Indians. Maybe Ohio would be as much fun as Hatboro.

"Used to be, anyway," said Daddy. "Wait till you get to our house, you'll see!"

"Indians?" said Jeffrey, wondering.

"Just wait and see," was all Daddy would say. Jeffrey couldn't help clapping his hands. He was sure there would be lots of interesting things in the new home. He remembered about the secret "if" he and Daddy had.

They stopped for lunch at one of the roadside parks that are placed so conveniently in Ohio. It was pleasant in the noon sunshine, and Aunt Ginny's picnic was very good. Everybody felt happy. After clearing away all signs of having eaten there, they went on their way feeling comfortable and ready for the rest of the journey.

It wasn't long till they came to Zanesville, which was quite a city.

"Is this Cincinnati?" Jeffrey asked.

"Not yet," Mother said, trying to keep Henry from pulling her to pieces.

"When will we come to Cincinnati?" Jeffrey asked again.

"We don't go right into Cincinnati," Mother explained patiently. "Our house is about twenty miles southeast of the city."

"Won't we even see it?" David seemed disappointed.

"Sometime," Mother said.

"Now I think it is time to look at the secrets. David, yours is the one in the corner. Jeffrey, yours is the large one. One of the soft ones is for Henry, and the other is for all of you."

Even before Mother had finished speaking, the boys were up on their knees, finding their own packages and pulling at the one that was for all of them, which they opened first.

"It's Halloween!" said David. "I'll bet the kids are having lots of fun back home."

"Today?" asked Jeffrey. "Well, we're having fun, too."

There was a tramp mask for Jeffrey, a Chinese one for David with a black crepe-paper cap and long braid. For Henry there was a smaller one like a Dutch doll.

David's package held a face made of cardboard with separate sets of eyes and noses. There were extra mouths, too, and different chins and mustaches. All kinds of different faces could be made with them.

Jeffrey's package held a book of pictures with perforated outlines. The pictures could be taken out without scissors, and bent and folded into barns and houses to make a village. There were people and animals, too.

When they had tired of laughing at the

funny faces, the boys set to work making the
paper houses and barns. For a long time there
was only the quietest talking on the back seat.
Daddy drove steadily, and the car went pur-
r-r, put-put, pur-r-r, put-put, over the road
that wound in and out, over and around, till
the hills were gone. Then it led straight ahead
over level ground for a long, long time.

White stone markers began to appear on

the road. David read "120 miles to Cincinnati." There was something else printed below, but David didn't see it in time. When they had gone a few miles farther, there was another marker like the first. This time David read the second direction. It said "48 miles to Washington C. H." What could Washington C. H. mean? Daddy didn't know. Mother didn't know. What could it mean?

All the way along, every two miles or so, there was another stone marker, and the distance was always less to "Washington C. H." How simple it seemed, when they finally came to the town, to see that it stood for Washington Court House.

"Of course," said Daddy. "The county seat."

"What's county seat?" asked Jeffrey.

Then Daddy explained how the states are

divided up into counties, and how each county is supposed to take care of its own roads and schools. There is a courthouse in each county, and the town where it stands is called the county seat.

It was dark when they came to the next big town, where they stopped for supper. Daddy brought milk from a store, and they ate sandwiches in the car. They started out again, turning south onto another road.

"When are we going to get to our house?" begged Jeffrey.

"How much longer is it?" David groaned.

Henry was not as happy as he had been, either. Mother held him tight in her arms, and soon he was fast asleep.

Jeffrey fell asleep, too. His nose was half buried in the pile of coats, his hand was on the tricycle, and his feet in David's lap. David didn't mind. He was asleep, too, his chin on his hand, his elbow on Jeffrey's hip.

Daddy drove on into the night, over the strange roads. They went through small towns, following the route numbers on the

signs, with Mother keeping track of the way by the map and flashlight. After leaving the main highway at Washington C. H., they had to change roads often in order to go as directly as possible to the house on the river. They met few cars, and the only light was from the stars. The last road was narrow and winding. Sometimes it went sharply up and sometimes suddenly down. Great hills rose, and they crossed and recrossed a creek. It seemed endless. Henry grew heavier and heavier. But they were almost at the end of their journey.

Suddenly Mother said, "There's the highway! I see cars passing."

"Right you are!" said Daddy. "I believe that's it. Now we have only to turn right, go a few hundred yards, and we are home." He sighed deeply.

As Daddy drove slowly, so as not to miss the house, the lights of other cars came into view and showed the way. There above, not a hundred yards away, on the hill, stood the house, white with green trim, all newly painted. Daddy drew in close to the side of the road to let fast-moving cars go by. Then he saw the mailbox. On the side of it was Daddy's name as plain as could be — A. KUHN.

Daddy laughed.

"That Bill," he said. "He has even planted our mailbox and put our name on it."

The boys woke up.

"Are we there?" David blinked sleepily.

"Are we at our house?" Jeffrey was wide awake all at once.

"House?" smiled Henry, waking up, too.

The driveway went almost straight up. Daddy had to put the car into low gear to get it up the hill and onto the level place beside the back door. The flashlight helped them to find the lock and the light switches.

"We're lucky to have had a friend like Bill to attend to all these things for us," said Daddy as the room sprang into light. It was bare and empty. The moving van had not arrived.

"What shall we do?" asked David.

"Where shall we sleep?" asked Jeffrey. "There aren't any beds."

"Just wait," said Daddy. "I think we have a way around that. Let's look upstairs first." Daddy led the way up the stairs, which were between the walls and went right up from the room they had first entered. Mother helped Henry, and they trooped up in a line after Daddy. He went into the largest room, and there, standing ready, were two new beds.

"Just what I hoped for," said Daddy. "Bill has seen to it that the beds are in place, and for one night we can manage without proper

bedding. Henry's crib is in the back of the car. In the morning the van will probably be here."

Every room had to be looked into, every light turned on, and every door opened. It was very exciting. Voices made a loud echoing noise in the empty house, and the new beds were springy to fall upon.

"Now to bed, every one of us. We have to be up and ready for the van in the morning."

4   When Jeffrey opened his eyes in the morning, he didn't know where he was. Then he remembered! The whole new home in Ohio — to explore — and today anything could happen — even Daddy's "if."

"Hurry up, David," he called. "Today will be fun."

The sun poured into every room except the kitchen and the study. There was a large room which had once been the kitchen but was now what Mother called the "utility room." It had a big cupboard for storing things and a place for laundry work. It was a fine place for playing, for sewing and ironing, and for Daddy's photographic equipment. A real "utility" room. The new kitchen was arranged in a smaller room that had once been a bedroom. All the cupboards were new. The sink and the stove were new, too, and the refrigerator Daddy had bought was in place. Everything was ready to use. Mother managed to get breakfast with what was left in the lunch basket. There was coffee in one thermos and milk in the other. There were no chairs or tables, so they had to sit on the floor. Mother said it was just like the kitchen-

90

floor picnic they'd had once when she was a girl.

"Our mother had promised that we could

have a picnic on the Fourth of July," she said. "But it happened to turn cold that day, and the wind blew. We had a new little baby brother, and Mother was afraid to take him out in the wind. Of course my sister and I were disappointed, so Mother promised that we should have the picnic anyway. She spread a cloth on the clean kitchen floor and set out the food just as if it had been in the park. It was lots of fun, just as this is."

"Fun?" said Henry, getting up from his place and putting his sandwich on his head.

After breakfast Daddy said the boys could go up the hill. But first he talked to them seriously.

"Boys," he said, "I want you to listen carefully. This road down below the house is a busy highway. Trucks and cars go over it from North Carolina away out West, and they

go very fast. It is winding, too, and very dangerous. You both know how to watch and cross only when it is safe. But that road is never to be crossed unless it is necessary. Henry doesn't know anything about roads and must never be allowed near it. Do you both understand?"

David and Jeffrey both nodded solemnly. When Daddy spoke in that way, they listened and obeyed. Daddy went on.

"You may go up the hill and play on our own ground all you please, but you may not go over the fence to the neighbors' without permission. You may climb our own trees and you may play in the barn and the corncrib if you promise to be careful and not do silly things. You know whether you are doing the right things or not, don't you?"

Both boys nodded again.

"All right," said Daddy.

Away went the boys, out of the door, up the steep side of the yard, along the stone wall across the back, up, up, up. The land belonging to the house went clear to the top of the hill.

Above the house and yard, higher than the tops of the trees, there was a level place which looked as if it had been a garden. From there the boys turned to look.

"Look!" cried Jeffrey. "It's the world!"

"We're above our roof!" marveled David. Far down the hill was the red tin roof of the house and the porch. Beyond were the tall trees in the front yard, and below that the highway. A cornfield stretched below the road, then rows of trees, and then—the Ohio River. It lay broad and silvery in the morning light, and beyond were hills again. They

were so far away they looked blue and hazy.
Smoke lay along the river where a toy train
ran, and far, far up on the crest of the hill
were tiny trees.

"Let's go farther up the hill," said David,

climbing the slippery path. "This is better than Hatboro." Beside the path were stones, filling a small gully where the water had raced down. Jeffrey picked one up to feel the weight of it. It was a curious shape, pointed at one end and squared off at the other. It looked somewhat like a hatchet head.

While the boys were examining it, they heard Daddy's shout from below. He came up to where they were standing.

"What have you found?" he asked, taking the stone from David to look at it.

"Aha! Indians! Didn't I tell you? This is a tomahawk. See the place where the thong bound it to the stick? There must be hundreds of Indian relics here."

Daddy was as excited as the boys. He went on a little way, pulling himself up by the seedling trees and bushes which grew thickly all

about. In another moment he picked up another stone. This time it was shaped a little like an arrowhead at one end and rounded at the other. It was rather flat and much smaller than the other one. There was a deep, rounded depression, which just fitted Jeffrey's finger, and a groove where it had been fastened to a stick.

"This must be a hatchet," said Daddy. "Look at the stone itself. You remember what I told you about the inland sea and the fossils? This stone is covered with fossils. All those little tiny circles and wavy lines were once small marine animals."

"What's marine?" asked Jeffrey.

"Anything to do with the sea," Daddy answered.

"Let's see what else there is." David was already on his way farther up the hill. Daddy stopped to pick up seed pods of different kinds. He stopped to look at the bark of unfamiliar trees. He plucked green shoots from the cedars and smelled of them. He pulled out dead branches as he went, and made a path through the tall grasses so Jeffrey could follow. David was out of sight. The hill was covered with a thick growth. There were honey locusts with long, sharp thorns; hickory, black walnut, and sycamore. Little by little Daddy and Jeffrey had worked their way up the hill, going on a slant to make it easier.

"I want to see what kind of oak tree this is," Daddy said. "If we can find the acorns, we can tell. You can always tell a tree by its seed." They had to break through a tangle of dead branches and thick, long grass. There was

98

another gully to cross, only much deeper than the first one. A half-hidden path wound steeply up, then leveled off to an open place.

"Let's see what's up here first," said Daddy. "Give me your hand." At the top of the rise they found a sunken grave with a headstone lying flat. Daddy raised it and scraped away the green moss and the earth until he could read the words:

HERMAN KREIDEL

Died Jan. 6, 1836
two years, three mos.

The budded rose
Has faded and died
But it blooms anew
On the other side.

"Oh," he said quietly, "a little boy not

much older than Henry."

"Oh," said Jeffrey, "a little buried boy." He felt very sad, thinking of the boy who was like little Henry.

"It was a long, long time ago," said Daddy. "Longer than when Grandpa was a little boy. Let's put the stone up straight and level the ground." He leaned it against a sapling. "We'll fix it better when I get some tools. Now we must go back to see what we can do for Mother. We've been gone long enough."

Just then David's head appeared over the grasses.

"Guess what!" called Jeffrey. "We've found a little buried boy!"

"Put your mouth!" said David.

Jeffrey stood straight and put his mouth.

"Where?" asked David, jumping down the last few feet. "Show me."

David couldn't read the worn letters, but
Jeffrey pointed to each word just as Daddy
had. It was almost as good as reading.

"Before we go down the hill," Daddy said, "we can look a little farther over here. There is a deep ravine that I seem to remember seeing when I was here before."

"Maybe there's bears!" said Jeffrey, as if he hoped there might be.

"I've been told there are foxes," Daddy said.

The ground began to drop down quickly. They came to a fence, and there, through the branches of a sycamore tree, they could see the ravine. It went down, down, as deep as a house. Along the sides and covering the bottom were great stones. There was no water, because, Daddy said, there had been a dry spell.

"There will be plenty of water when the rains come in a month or two," he said. "This is one place where you mustn't go," he added.

"You might not be able to get out again. Remember."

Coming down and across the hill again, Daddy pointed out the orchard above the barn. They stopped for a moment on the level place to look again at the wide-spreading view and the rooftop of the house.

"Those hills beyond the river are in Kentucky," said Daddy.

"What's Kentucky?" Jeffrey wanted to know.

"Kentucky's another state," David said.

"That's right, another state," Daddy explained. "Like Ohio and Pennsylvania and West Virginia."

It just looked like the whole world to Jeffrey. Then he shouted, "Look! The moving men are here! Whee!" He bounced down the hill, taking giant leaps over the hummocky ground, with David after him, and Daddy following.

The men were just unloading the boys' beds and desk when they came down the last stretch of the hill. The van was half empty. The boys tore into the house to see how it looked with furniture in it. Their voices and heavy shoes still echoed, but already the sound was different, and somewhat muffled by the furniture. The old, familiar desk that had been great-grandmother's looked quite at home against the strange wall. The bookshelves stood empty and waiting to be filled, but on top of them were the lamp and the fruit bowl, just as they had always stood. There was a pile of rugs in the middle of the floor. The boys took turns jumping on them till Mother came in and shooed them outdoors again.

"Go on out again," she said. "You will only get in the way of the men. Go see what else you can discover." She bustled about, moving small things into place and settling chairs out of the way. Henry was in his pen on the back porch.

"Remember what Daddy said about being careful!" she called as the boys ran out.

"We will!"

"The barn!" said both boys at once, racing off down the slope.

Part of the barn stood right on the road, but the hill rose so steeply that the upper part of it was on another level. Where the boys went into it, they found themselves on the second floor. There was a great opening from that part into the hayloft, and a great yawning hole down to the lower level. Jeffrey drew back and held onto David. It was a little scary.

David held on tight to the side of the shed while they looked into the big barn. There wasn't much to see. The barn hadn't been used for years. Shafts of light came through the slits between the boards. Great timbers stretched across empty space, and uprights still stood where there had been stalls for horses or cows.

"Hey!" said David, but softly, because he was still a little awed by the bigness of the barn. "I see where we could build a house. There's lots of boards and things. Maybe Daddy will let us."

Jeffrey wanted to get away from the big hole.

"Let's go see what else there is," he said. There was more to see. There was a large chicken house, and a tool shed, and, best of all, a corncrib. It had a little window in the side that was a fine place for playing elevator. There was a half ladder lying in the weeds, and boxes to stand on. David found a rope hanging inside the barn shed. A paint-covered

bucket lay among the trash that had been left, and in no time at all the boys had rigged the elevator. They had so much fun that before they knew it, it was noon and Mother was calling them to come to lunch.

"Home!" said Jeffrey. "This is home, isn't it? Daddy, am I going to — you know what?" He clapped his hands under his chin.

Daddy laughed. "We'll see," he said. "After lunch we'll go in to the village for supplies." He leaned toward Jeffrey and touched his arm. "Then we'll see," he said. "But it is only 'if,' you know."

After lunch, Daddy took the two boys with him in to the village. They craned their necks to look up as they rode along, because the hill rose straight up from the road. There were houses here and there. Every so often they crossed a road and then a stream coming down through the hills. David read the signs each time as they passed: NINE MILE ROAD — TEN MILE ROAD.

"These creeks all run into the river," Daddy explained. "That's what makes it the big river."

Then the boys crowded to the other side of the car to look out at the river. Just here they could see the river from the road. It looked wide and deep.

"Sometimes the river overflows, after heavy rains," said Daddy. "Then the road is covered and nobody can pass."

"How will you go to work in Cincinnati?" asked Jeffrey.

"How will I go to school?" wondered David.

"I made sure of a way," said Daddy, "before taking the house. There is a road high up above the water line. We have to go up the hill behind the house to get to it."

"Wouldn't it be fun to see the road all covered with water!"

"Not much fun for the people whose houses are flooded," said Daddy. "They have to move up onto the second floor, or leave altogether."

They drove in to the village, and Daddy
left the boys while he went on an errand.
There was a great barge coming slowly down
the river toward them. Jeffrey wondered if it
could be the one they had seen when they
had crossed into Ohio on their way to the
new home.

When Daddy came back he was smiling. He was smiling right at Jeffrey.

"You know what? It is no longer 'if' — it is 'yes'," he said. "You can go to school with David. The bus will stop at our door about five minutes of eight. You will stay all day and be brought back at four in the afternoon."

"Really?" said Jeffrey, unbelieving. "Put your mouth!"

Daddy "put his mouth" and said, "Really. The school is not too crowded."

"Do we have to go now, right away?" David questioned. He didn't look as happy as Jeffrey. He wasn't sure he wanted to go to a new school. He wondered what his new teacher would be like. Would she be pleasant like Miss Torrey? Would there be books to read?

The next morning, very early, Jeffrey was

up and dressed, his face shining, his hair wet and slick. The parting in it looked somewhat like a rail fence. David was up early, too, and together the boys whispered and tiptoed so they wouldn't wake Henry. Daddy and Mother were downstairs getting breakfast. Already the lunches were packed.

"This first day you will have to buy milk," said Mother. "Afterward we'll get lunch kits so you can carry it."

"Remember what I told you about being careful," said Daddy. "Stand on the steps till you see the bus, then look both ways before you cross."

Jeffrey was so excited he could hardly eat any breakfast. He was ready long before David who came dashing down the walk. They stood on the little platform halfway down the bank. Mother stood on the porch,

watching. "Remember to look," she said.

They waited for a few moments. Cars passed, going and coming. The boys saw the yellow school bus coming around the curve. They looked to the left. Nothing was in sight. They looked to the right. Nothing was coming except the bus. They ran down the steps and across the road. They stood waiting. The bus came along and stopped. It was full of boys and girls of all ages. Some of them smiled at David and Jeffrey. Mother waved from the top of the steps. Jeffrey was on his way to school.

That night, after supper, the whole family sat on the steps of the front porch, eating apples. It was warm for November. It was note quite dark, so they could see the line of the Kentucky hills lying in blue mist above the river.

"How was school?" Mother asked David. "Did you like it?"

Yes," David nodded. "It's a good school, and they have a library where I can get books to read. I can even bring them home!"

"Did you like school, too?" asked Mother, turning to Jeffrey.

"Of course," said Jeffrey. "Didn't you?"

"Of course," said Mother. "What is your teacher like?"

"She's pretty," said Jeffrey. "She calls me Sugarlump."

David pointed at Jeffrey and taunted him.

"Baby Sugarlump! Baby Sugarlump!"

But Jeffrey didn't mind. Mother often called him Honey — so what was the difference?

He was in the first grade. That was really important.

"Look!" he said, pointing to the big tree which stood where the lawn dropped down to the road.

"Look, there's a whole house and a barn and trees and everything right in the crotch of that tree."

"So there is," said Mother. "It's so far away. It looks very small."

"It looks like the houses under Grandma's Christmas tree," said David. "And just think! It's in another state. Daddy says it's Kentucky over there."

"We can see the whole world," said Jeffrey, "and one house." Then he thought about the wide world they had seen from up the hill. He wondered if there might be a little boy living in that far house in Kentucky. If he did live there, could he look through this same tree? Could he see this house in Ohio? Would it look small and far, far away, too? Could he see the whole world from the top of his hill? He wondered.

His front tooth felt looser than it had before. He put his finger to his mouth.

When he touched it, the loose tooth

dropped in his hand.

"Look!" he cried. "My front tooth fell out, just like David's did that time."

"Put your mouth!" said David.

Jeffrey had to grin. But even if he couldn't "put his mouth," the grin spoke for him. Where his tooth had been there was a wide gap. David grinned, too. He remembered how big he had felt when he had lost his first tooth.

Jeffrey sighed happily. Tomorrow he would go to school again. He would take his lunch, just like David. He would stay all day, just like David. He would learn more letters, and soon he would know how to read, just like David. When school was over, he and David would come home from the world to one house. This house. Home.

STOP!
SCHOOL
BUS
#415